Misinformed

By Josh "Mode" Ford

This publication contains the opinions and ideas of its author. It is intended to provide helpful and informative material on the subjects addressed in the publication. The author and publisher specifically disclaim all responsibility for any liability, loss, or risk, personal or otherwise, that is incurred as a consequence, directly or indirectly of the use or application of any of the contents of this book.

<u>Dedicated to You, the Reader</u>

__Cannon Castell, Aurthur Ramsey, Leo Enoch__

www. OutTheCage.Com

Table of Contents

Bottom Line: The Reason

Chapter 1: Intro: Game Time

Chapter 2: Coaches' Meeting

Chapter 3: Monday Practice

Chapter 4: Benched

Chapter 5: Breaking & Entering

Chapter 6: Court

Chapter 7: Community Service

Chapter 8: Day 1: Who Are You?

Chapter 9: Day 2: The Real Bench

Chapter 10: Different Types of Athletes

Chapter 11: Day 3: Character Matters

Chapter 12: Day 4: Sacrifice

Chapter 13: Day 5: Athletics & Academics

Chapter 14: Chalk Talk: Visions vs. Hallucinations

Chapter 15: Support & Redemption

Pro Huddle

<u>Bottom Line: The Reason</u>

The news and media outlets constantly remain
crammed with stories of misinformed athletes
making terrible decisions and often hurting others
or themselves, in addition to harming the
reputations of their schools and professional
organizations. As athletes, we are a part of a very
exclusive group. Often times, as athletes, we are
ultra focused on winning, on uniforms, on
highlights, and on skill development. We forget our
own holistic development and personal
improvement. Very few of us see success outside
of athletics.

Most of us are misinformed around the longevity of
sports, misinformed about the probability of
athletics. We are therefore perfectly set up to
hallucinate.

We devalue things that can help create true value.
And we miss out on a proper valuation of learning.

Hear me now… There is nothing wrong with
competing, winning, aspirations of going pro,
ambitions to break records—and goals to simply be
the best. Hear me once more… Do it! Win games,
compete, win championships and train hard!!
However, understand that playing a sport isn't a
career—it's an experience.

Be the best but take advantage of *every* opportunity
you're given and maximize them. Use sports as a
vehicle to take you places, don't let sports use you.
Make sure you're developing in all areas of life.

Chapter 1

Intro: Game Time

The stadium was jam-packed with nothing but pure energy in the atmosphere. Hundreds of people from all over the state showed up to see the most talked about sophomore sensation in the nation. They came to see Quarterback Zane Thompson and the Virgil T. High School Falcons football team battle the Fort Morgan Bobcats on a cold Friday night underneath the lights. It was a home game for the Falcons and it was a sellout event. Though it was only a high school game, the status of the game was extraordinary and so was the atmosphere around it. The stadium was loud; the smell of fresh turf, hot coco, nachos and BBQ filled the air.

This was an important game for both teams, it was week six of the football season and both were undefeated.

The history of this game went back to the year 1982, which was the first year the rivalry started, and since then, it was a meaningful game each year. Virgil T. High School was one of the top schools in the city with tons of tradition, yet in recent years, the football program hadn't been doing so well. Nevertheless, this year thus far, they were 6-0 for the first time in a really long time.

Zane was only a sophomore, but he was one of the top players in the state. Heck, he was one of the top players in the entire country. Prep websites, fan websites, blog sites and even all the credible scout/recruiting sites evaluated and tagged him as "The Future." They also gave him nice ratings across the board due to his tremendous skills. This all meant he was a top high school prospect from coast to coast, and he was destined to be not only a college-bound phenom, but also a professional athlete one day.

On this night, Zane was having a good game. He was balling out despite his team's being down by three scores.

Zane was starting on both offense and defense for the Falcons. He was playing well but the team was having some struggles. He pretty much carried the load. Though he was a just a sophomore, it was *no excuses!* Zane had to play a big role in order for his team to be victorious. From a fan perspective, the game had been outstanding; the crowd was truly observing a great matchup. The third quarter was quickly coming to an end. Zane and the Falcons were down and needed a huge play. They were on offense; everyone watched as Zane stood in the backfield waiting to take the snap. Watching him in the backfield was like watching your favorite superhero get ready to defeat the bad guy—you just knew something amazing was coming.

He went through his cadence, "Ready, ready, blue 18, blue 18, set hit." The ball was snapped. Zane dropped back, going through his progression.

A Bobcat defensive lineman broke through the line, applying instant pressure. Zane was able to elude him, then juke another Bobcat defender, escaping the defensive pressure. He fired a nice deep pass to his receiver Mike Wilson. It was a good-looking accurate 60-yard bomb. Mike caught it in stride and was off to the races. He scored a touchdown. The stadium erupted, going wild. After the made extra point, the score was now 28-14, the Bobcats still led. Following the touchdown and extra point with perfect timing, the D.J. in the booth played "We Ready." The energy of the game was definitely changing. The crowed was hyped and the Falcons were closing the margin on the game.

The clock went to zero and the third quarter ended with a huge bang from the Falcons. Zane and his teammates were pumped. Looking at the scoreboard, they were one score closer to catching up and possibly winning this game. As the fourth quarter began, everyone in the stadium was on their feet and both teams continued playing hard.

Throughout the entire fourth quarter, Zane and his teammates made plays, and the Bobcats made huge plays as well. They both were getting giant stops. It was a back and forth battle. As time was winding down, it was the Falcons who were able to get a stop and score once more on the same exact bomb pass play to Mike Wilson, but this time it was an 80-yard pass instead of 60 yards. Following the made extra point, the score was now 28-21. The Falcon fans were jumping and yelling with excitement.

After the Falcons' Mike Wilson touchdown, the Bobcats got the ball back; they didn't want to lose this game either. They were just as hungry and willing to do what it takes in this game. The Bobcats were the top team in the state for 6 consecutive years. Although historically they had always had trouble when playing against the Virgil T. High Falcons, they had been running through them in the last couple of years. In addition to leading the rivalry, the Bobcats had also won the last six state championships.

They were simply a super powerhouse their superlative tradition added to the importance of this game.

The Bobcats were marching down the field ready to score. Zane stood on defense waiting for them to break their huddle and line up. You see, when Zane wasn't on offensive playing quarterback, he was on defense as a defensive back, specifically safety. His responsibility was to never let anything ever get past him—and to hit opponents hard. His speed and God-given talent allowed him to make plays everywhere.

The Bobcats Quarterback, Tim Stevenson, went through his cadence breathing really hard, "Ready, ready, set hit." He took the snap and handed the ball off to his running back, Tre Moore. Tre made a nice move, breaking through the line as he juked the linebacker. Then he was tackled from behind and lost the football as it went bouncing like a rock skipping across a lake.

Out of nowhere, scooping the ball up from his safety position, was none other than Zane. He was so fast, all he could think of was, "I have to score."

Zane could hear his head coach, Coach McAllister, and half the sideline, shout, "Go score, go score. Score!" He quickly ran left and was greeted by a host of Bobcat players. But he was able to reverse field like a mongoose fleeing a group of snakes. He sprinted the opposite way, eluding defenders and getting amazing blocks from his teammates. He broke down the sideline towards the end zone with only one person to beat—and that was Bobcats quarterback Tim Stevenson. As Tim tried to tackle Zane, he was met with a ferocious stiff arm as Zane dashed down the sideline, taking the interception back for a Falcon touchdown. The crowed once again went crazy. The Fort Morgan side was completely shocked. However, after the touchdown, the Falcons kicker, Dakota Wilson, missed the extra point field goal. The score was 28-27; the Falcons were literally down by a point.

Coach McAllister and the Falcons opted to kick an onside kick to get the ball back.

The crowd was completely silent as they watched anxiously. When both teams lined up, the stadium was so silent you could hear a penny drop. This was a critical play. The Falcons lined up and the Bobcats were ready. Dakota was focused, even after missing the field goal. The ref blew the whistle, and Dakota kicked the ball. It went ricocheting, bouncing and hitting a Bobcats player in the chest before it rolled right back to the Falcons as their kicking coverage team swarmed and recovered the ball.

YEAAAHHH!!!! Shouted several Falcon players The crowd was even more electrified than they previously had been—supporters cheering, both sides pumped up.

History was being made, regardless, because this game had turned into a heart-stopping battle.

Only 27 seconds left in the game and Zane had the ball in his possession—with the game on the line. This is where great players are made. He stood in the backfield, scanning the defense. They had been tenacious all night.

Coach wanted Zane to run a sprint right option *"All Go to Mike."* Zane shook his head slightly, "No." He wanted to run a 28-toss throwback pass. Coach signaled in the play *"Sprint Right Option All Go"* (this was a rollout deep pass play). Zane ignored his coach and changed the play in the huddle. *"28-toss Throwback Pass,"* he said. He was confident this play would work. As he took the snap from the center, there was a bad exchange on the toss and the ball was fumbled. While everyone scrambled to cover it, Zane went to cover the ball, but was blasted by the defense. A Bobcats linebacker was able to jump on the ball. That fast, in a blink of an eye, on a blown play it was—game over.

Zane stood still in disbelief. This was the team's first loss of the season. He hated losing. He knew he could have made that play. He began blaming his running back he'd tossed it to for a bad toss back exchange. But it was really Zane's fault.

Coach Jack came over and asked, "What happened?"

Zane snapped at him instantly, "Man, shut up." Everyone stood around upset and confused.

All of a sudden, like a baby who hadn't been fed, Zane erupted. A lot of athletes who are superstars like Zane often forget that they're humans first. Zane had been soaked up in entitlement and the praises of others. He felt invincible so invincible he could push a coach.

He ran over to the sidelines cursing and yelling at everyone. "Coaches are dumb! Weak A** Team, Yall suck, Im transferring!

Coach Lue, the wide receivers' coach, ran over to Zane to try and deescalate things. "Zane, we'll bounce back next week. Stay positive—and keep your head up," Coach Lue told him. He explained that this wasn't the end; the team would bounce back.

Zane wasn't ready to hear any of that. He shoved Coach Lue hard and shouted, "Nah, this team is dumb and yall coaches are dumb."
This wasn't the first time Zane had lashed out at teammates or disrespected coaches. He kept doing it, however, because he was so good and so athletic, he didn't see anything wrong with it—and honestly, he was never truly corrected or disciplined for anything.

Angry and distraught, Zane entered the locker room and turned confrontational, badmouthing both teammates and coaches. The hostility spilled out into the hallways. School security was called. Admin and parents who heard it all were stunned.

After a while, though, everything eventually calmed down.

The ugly news of Zane's actions had reached Coach Justin as he was walking down from the press box following a post-game interview. Coach Justin was the first-year quarterback coach and co-offensive coordinator. He was actually the one who called the *"Sprint RT Option play"* that Zane had declined to run. Coach Justin was always in the press box during the games, never on the sideline like other coaches. He was the one who spent the most time with Zane when it came to football. A parent ran up to him and said, "Coach, you better get your boy— he's tripping!"

Coach Justin took a deep breath; he already knew that they were talking about Zane. He made his way to the locker room where he found Zane and asked him, "What's going on?"

Zane rudely ignored him and walked away. Coach tried to give Zane the benefit of the doubt, thinking maybe it was because of the loss, but he knew something bad had taken place.

He honestly was fed up with Zane's entitled behavior and attitude. He knew the kid was special, though. Coach proceeded to ask one of the football team's captains, senior offensive lineman, Jerry Williams, whose locker was right across from Zane's. "Jerry, good game out there tonight, man. But what's happened? What's going on in here?"

Jerry took a deep breath and responded, "Coach, it was so bad, I can't even repeat what was said."

At this moment Coach Justin was furious. As if the loss wasn't enough, he had to deal with self-inflicted wounds of the team. He had to deal with Zane's attitude and his trying to fight everyone. The problem wasn't the fact Zane was mad because of the loss; we all don't like losing and we all get mad in life. It was the fact that this was reoccurring behavior from Zane. Plain and simple, it was the way he conducted himself. He always behaved as if he was above the team, staff and everyone.

This was the breaking point for Coach Justin. He stood in the hallway, trying to figure out what to do next—in addition to calming his nerves.

Chapter 2

Coaches' Meeting

All the coaches gathered in the coach's office after each game. The head coach, Coach McAllister would always debrief as the rest of the coaches would join him, reflecting on the game that was just played. Afterwards, they'd look forward to the upcoming opponent. This game vs. the Bobcats was the first loss of the season, so the room was encased in silence, much different from the previous weeks. They were all shocked but quickly recognized there were more games and more of the season to be played.

Coach McAllister stood up and told everyone, "This one is my fault. Don't worry—we'll get better and learn from this loss."

All the other coaches replied, "Nah, coach, it's all of us."

Coach Justin just stood in a corner of the office, looking up at the ceiling, processing everything that was taking place. Coach McAllister opened up the floor to anyone who wanted to speak or had any comments on the game.

Coach Justin gently asked, "What happened?"

Coach McAllister replied, "We got to hold on to the ball. We'll do more exchange drills for sure."

"No, Coach, I meant after the game—with Zane," Coach Justin replied.

Simultaneously, all the coaches, including Coach Lue who had been pushed, responded, "Nothing, it's just football; it's a part of the game."

Coach Justin gave every one of his coaches the "are you serious?" look.

Suddenly, Coach Lue said, "He got a little worked up, Justin, but I like a guy like that."

"Punching your teammates, cussing and pushing coaches, cussing out parents—you like that?" Coach Justin responded. "His behavior has been an issue and his habits have been the same, but we cover it up. He's barely in class, but somehow is passing them all." I see what's going on. He thought to himself, *"Why does nobody else seem to be disappointed with Zane's behavior?"*

Coach McAllister broke it down for Justin. "Look, Coach, this isn't the little recreation center you run. This is football. The kid will be fine; he just got a little upset."

Coach Justin didn't like that at all. He left the room and went home.

Later that night, although he was very upset, he went back in and watched film of the game. As he was watching, his mood began to change.

He was torn because Zane had a good game against the Bobcats. Zane was lights out and he graded out really well. His numbers were outstanding and the kid was a true baller.

Coach got through the entire game and graded out Zane with an A-. (Your game grade reflects how well you played, and an A- was amazing.) Coach knew Zane had a great game, but his conduct was way beyond poor. He spent the rest of the weekend working at his center while getting his mind off the loss.

Chapter 3

Monday Practice

That Monday, Coach Justin made his way to the coaching office before heading to the team meeting. Mondays were the days that the entire team would all come together in the team room and watch the full tape of the previous Friday game on the projector. Coach walked into the fieldhouse excited for another week. He decided to let the episode go with Zane, thinking to himself, _"The boy's young; he'll learn."_ However, as he was walking, he passed the trainer's room and ran into Mindy, one of the student athletic trainers. She had a fretted look on her face. He asked her, "Umm, what's wrong, Mindy?"

Mindy didn't say anything; she just took her phone out. She showed him a social media post from Zane. It said, "Real talk, my coaches are stupid man-". He also was being disrespectful while going "live" on social media.

Coach Justin became upset all over again. He knew that a lot of people (especially kids) use social media to vent and carry on about stuff, but Zane wasn't like a lot of people. He had all eyes on him. Disheartened, Coach marched out of the training room and went to find Zane.

Zane was hanging in the locker room with some friends. Coach Justin approached him and said, "Hey Zane, come holla at me."

"Nah, I'm busy right now," Zane responded in a condescending tone.

Shocked, Coach Justin walked out of the locker room.

Chapter 4

Benched

The team gathered in the team room, and the meeting began. Coach Justin was running the meeting. "How's everyone doing?" he asked.

"Great, Coach," the team replied.

"I know this last game hurt but we got another big game coming up this week; it's time to refocus and get back on track," he said. He went to the board and illustrated the schemes, the plays, the game plan and the personnel for the team's upcoming game against the Lakewood Wolves. Surprisingly, Coach Justin didn't have Zane in the lineup at all. Like, not only was he not starting, he wasn't in the lineup at all!

The team room was silent. All the players had a look of concentration as they watched Coach on the board, but inside, each player was really confused and shocked about Zane not being up there.

A couple of players glanced at Zane to see his reaction. He sat unbothered. He had a grin on his face; he wasn't taking coach seriously at all. All the other coaches were speechless as well—for the simple fact that this hadn't been discussed at all.

They didn't know how to react. Coach Justin shouted, "Kane! You ready? You're starting at quarterback this week. Thomas! You'll be backing him up." Kane was a junior backup quarterback; he was an amazing athlete and a great kid. Thomas was a senior who was also pretty good. Neither of them was as athletic as Zane, though they could definitely play.

Kane looked shocked and puzzled. He stuttered a little bit before he responded, "I'm ready coach." Coach Justin continued the meeting, going over the game plan. Zane was texting on his phone (which wasn't supposed to be in the meeting) and completely tuned out, not even paying attention at all.

All the other coaches were bothered but masked their emotions as if everything was okay. In their minds, they needed Zane to play.

The team meeting let out.

Following it, the head coach, Coach McAllister, called a mandatory coaches meeting. He was furious. All the coaches gathered in the coach's office. It was silence for a few minutes. Coach McAllister shouted, "Justin what the heck are you doing? You're not benching Zane!"

"His actions need to be punished. He owes the team and us coaches an apology," Coach Justin responded.

"He doesn't owe us sh*t but wins and to keep balling out," replied Coach McAllister.

The defensive coordinator Coach Wilks chimed in, "I'll say this, you can bench him or whatever you want on the offensive side of the ball, but you better believe he's starting on defense."

Coach Justin shouted "I'd rather lose with good character guys, than win with that type of selfishness. Honestly, what type of young men are we developing? I'm tired of it only being about the wins; we have an obligation to help these boys become better men."

We have an obligation to win State," said Coach Lue.

"He's starting at quarterback—and that's the end of it," said Head Coach McAllister.

A huge silence fell over the office.

Coach Justin paused for a second, shocked at the coaching staff and the things they were saying. Coach Justin stood and said, "Well then I'm resigning."

"Come on coach, don't do this," said Coach Lue as Justin turned around and left the office.

"No, let him go," said Coach Wilks.

Coach Justin hurried to the parking lot, got in his truck, and took off. He was saddened at what took place in that office. He loved being a coach at Virgil

T. High School; he loved his players, but he couldn't take it anymore.

He drove home flabbergasted, asking himself, *"Do coaches care about the personal development of athletes? Or are they just worried about themselves and their own agenda—are they just worried about winning and themselves?"*

Coach Justin wasn't like the other coaches. He wasn't in it for just the "X's and O's" but also for the "Jimmy and Joes." He used sports as an opportunity to help young boys become men and to help them become better people.

Coach Justin dedicated his life to helping others. He actually founded the Sara Smith Center. The Sara Smith Center was a center where all the kids in the community spent their time. It was open from 3:00 to 9:00 in the evening. It was an outlet and a safe haven for the community. The population it served was all kids ages 6-18. The center offered activities such as sports, games, art, a computer lab, learning room, teen center and more. Outside of football, that's the place where you'd catch Coach spending and investing all his time.

He resigned and the season went on.

Chapter 5

Breaking & Entering

The very next day around 1:00 pm Zane and his friend Samuel Jones were driving around, cruising the city. Zane was ditching school, something he did pretty often, and Samuel, who was a basketball standout, had been kicked out of school. Zane should have been in class, but his parents and coaches could care less as long as he did the bare minimum, but put up great numbers. He was that good. The entitlement factor and privileged mindset were in full rotation.

Samuel was a senior. He was one of the best athletes the city had seen. A true hooper, Samuel could do it all on the basketball court. He went to Westview High School, but earlier in the year, he had gotten expelled for getting caught with drugs. Samuel was the truth on the court.

As a sophomore he averaged 25 points a game, and last year in his junior season, he averaged 31 points per game. He literally did it all and was rated a five-star recruit.

This year he planned to do the same, but his dismissal from the team and his expulsion were painful, even though it was his own fault. Samuel was highly misinformed when it came to sports and life. He lacked balance, and after previously getting in trouble for multiple fights, smoking, and theft, Westview High was tired of his shenanigans.

Samuel and Zane were riding around in the Mapleton Hills Area, one of the richest communities in the entire state. Maple Hills had luxury houses, nice cars, and just overall beauty. It's where all the rich people lived, far away from where Samuel and Zane were from.

They would often come to Mapleton Hills to dream.

They would visualize and dream about living in those mansions and driving in those cars when they make it to the top.

They dreamed that when they make to the NBA and NFL, they were going to move to Mapleton Hills, buy their moms houses, and much more. Ironically, no professional ball players lived in Mapleton Hills; it was filled with lawyers, engineers, doctors, and many people with inherited wealth.

Samuel would sneak off to the area quite often because he had a car. He'd come to fantasize about "Living Large," and he would also come to break into people's houses and steal. Time after time, he would come up on big money and nice electronics.

On this day, Samuel and Zane were riding around in Mapleton Hills when Samuel noticed that a lot of the residents weren't home. Samuel was experienced; he could scope out the perfect house to break into.

He looked at Zane and asked, "Are you down?"

Without hesitation, Zane said, "Hell, yea."

The afternoon was peaceful. It was a beautiful day. All you could hear and feel was the nice cool breeze. Most of the houses were empty; it seemed like everyone was either out of town or at work. Samuel chose a random house to hit.

The two parked a block away from the house. "This is a good spot. Let's get in and get out," Samuel directed.

The two crept into the backyard. Samuel popped the backdoor open and they entered the house. He said, "I'll go upstairs; you stay on the main level."

Samuel rushed upstairs as Zane stayed down on the main level. They quickly began to search the house. You could tell these homeowners loved sports and were true fanatics because of all the pictures, decorations and memorabilia they had displayed.

Samuel was able to grab jewelry and money from the master bedroom. Zane couldn't find anything at first, but then saw a Laptop on the dining room table. He grabbed it and put it in his backpack.

Zane was ready to go, but Samuel got greedy and wanted to search for more.

"Come on, man, let's go!" Zane lightly shouted.

All of a sudden, they heard steps from the basement. This was a huge house. Originally the two boys figured they were all alone, but that wasn't the case at all. The footsteps got closer; the two boys hid quickly.

Coming up the stairs was John Richardson. John was the son of the wealthy homeowners, Colin and Elizabeth Richardson. They were out of town on a business trip, so their son John was the only one home at the time. Coincidently, John himself had been a standout football player in high school.

He played receiver and was an All-American. Most recently, he was in college on a full ride scholarship, but was kicked out during his first semester for fighting and multiple team violations.

Most notably, John and a friend beat up a guy outside a bar. Then, in addition to that, when he was arrested, the cops found heavy drugs on him. John was suspended indefinably from the team and kicked out of school. He could have been a great asset to his team and possibly a great professional player, but his potential was wasted. It was a sad situation. Luckily, his father was in the oil business, and John was back living at home, learning about the family business. Not all athletes get such a second chance.

John had no idea Zane and Samuel were in the house. As he got to the top of the stairs, though, he noticed that the back door was open. He walked around the house and began to notice things had been rifled through and shuffled around. He yelled,

"Alright, I'm going to give you to the count of three to come out."

Samuel and Zane popped out.

All of a sudden, Samuel pushed John as he and Zane sprinted out of the house. They ran in opposite directions.

Shaken up, John dashed after the two. Furious, he chased after Samuel. Being an All-American in football, Player of the Year, and also ex-Division One receiver, John was able to catch Samuel and throw him to the ground. Samuel was surprised that he was caught. He shouted, "I'm sorry, my bad, my bad, here, here, here take it" as he tossed the jewelry and money he'd stolen. He was able to slip away from John and ran towards the car. He jumped in and sped off while calling Zane on his cellphone. Zane was already a few blocks away, and Samuel rushed to pick him up. The two got out of town ASAP.

As John walked back to his house, his heart was beating fast. He was bleeding but nothing too drastic.

He thought about letting the incident slide. He'd never met Zane or Samuel a day in his life, but he knew who they were (athletes can't hide). At first, he wasn't going to report the incident.

However, when he returned home and found his laptop and more items missing, he immediately called the police. The incident was also captured on the neighbor's outside cameras. Zane and Samuel had been caught; they just didn't know it yet.

They returned to Virgil T. High right as school got out, just before football practice. Zane went to practice and did his thing. Later, that night as they sat in the car outside Zane's house, they both laughed at the incident. "Why you give him the money back?" Zane said, laughing.

"Ha-ha aye, man, desperate times call for desperate measures," Samuel replied.

The two sat back and talked for hours. The only thing that mattered to them was ball. They neglected everything else because ball was life. They weren't bad, just miseducated. Since young ages, they believed that if they were good at sports, nothing else was important—and who's to blame them? People would worship them.

A lot of people did worship them, too. So, of course, all they knew was that ball is life.

The following the morning was bright and beautiful. Zane woke up and got ready for school. He tossed on his fresh CelosSportwear outfit and hit the door. When he arrived at school, Mr. Steward, the Dean of Students, met him as soon as he walked in the school building. Mr. Steward was the only person in the school who stayed on top of everyone and treated everyone (athletes and non-athletes) equally. He held everyone accountable. He was the least liked person in school, but he was the realest. He hated the leeway and privilege that the athletes received in school, especially Zane.

"Mr. Thompson, how are you this morning? Missed you yesterday." Mr. Steward greeted Zane.

"I'm splendid, Mr. Steward. Got to get to my locker."

"I missed you yesterday, didn't see you at all," Mr. Steward continued. "I have a surprise for you in my office. Let's take a walk."

Zane rolled his eyes and took a deep breath; he knew he was most likely getting written up or going to receive detention. He thought his teachers covered for him. His teachers loved the sports teams; they gave the best athletes passes all the time. Zane knew he would get the principal or someone to excuse him, though, so he wasn't worried. He just didn't like dealing with Mr. Steward.

As they arrived at Mr. Steward's office, Zane sat down. Within a few seconds of his sitting down, two men walked up behind him.

As Zane turned around, all he heard was, "Zane Thompson, you are under arrest." It was the police! They issued a warrant for his arrest for yesterday's burglary with Samuel. Zane tried to run but was blocked in. It didn't help that Mr. Steward's office was so small, almost like a phone booth. Zane surrendered and went with the officers. They went through the back of the school so nobody would notice, but Zane's arrested caused a big uproar, especially with the administration and the coaches. Everyone was puzzled and some didn't believe he had done it.

He was bonded out immediately but had to go to court in a few days.
Zane's mother didn't think he could do any wrong, so she didn't hold him accountable. Everyone blamed it on Samuel. "I don't want you hanging out with him anymore, baby—you're a future pro," his mom cried out.

Chapter 6

Court

Friday came around and it was time for court. Zane arrived and instantly felt awful when he saw his mother going through the metal detectors and being searched while entering the courthouse. However, he told himself, "I'll make it up to her when I go pro."

The courtroom was cold and insensitive. Zane wasn't worried at all, though. He assumed since he was a star, that nothing would happen to him and to make things more interesting, there were also three other star high school athletes in court that day. You had Dahl James there. Dahl was a star lacrosse standout arrested for domestic violence. Harmony Williams was also there. She was one of the top high school girls' basketball players in the nation.

She was arrested for disorderly conduct. She was always fighting in public or running with the wrong crowd despite being such an amazing athlete.

Top baseball prospect Cole Hughes was also in court; he was being accused of sexual misconduct. He was on track to be drafted, but even as an amateur, he could never make it through a season without being affected by off-field self-inflicted issues. Lastly, you had Samuel and Zane facing charges for burglary. Zane was present at court, but Samuel was nowhere to be found. As the hearings moved along, Zane kept looking at the door, waiting for Samuel to show up, but he never did. The result of this was that the judge put a warrant out for Samuel's arrest. He was in big trouble!

Things were miraculously moving in Zane's favor—the district attorney on the case was late, and Samuel didn't show up at all. Both of these circumstances happened to have an optimistic effect on Zane's case.

Judge Galloway had some background information
on Zane. He admitted to having seen him on
television and claimed he saw something in him.
Judge Galloway was also an alum of Virgil T. High
School. He felt badly for Zane because he'd seen so
many amazing athletes go down the wrong path;
now Zane was heading in that same direction.

The court let Zane choose the Diversion Program.
This program in the criminal justice system is a
form of sentencing in which the criminal
offender joins a program designed to help remedy
the behavior leading to the original arrest and then
allows the offender to avoid conviction and/or
a criminal record. Zane's being sentenced to this
program would mean he could keep a clean record
and learn from this incident while doing community
service. He would have to do community service
and pay restitution for the laptop he stole.

Needless to say, Zane pretty much got hit with a
slap on the wrist. He avoided jail. He gave a slight

grin after hearing his sentence. Then slickly said, "Thank you, Your Honor."

Judge Galloway firmly replied, "Let me go on record and say this, Mr. Thompson." (Zane quickly froze in shock.) The judge continued, "Mr. Thompson, a sentence to the diversion/community service program may seem like you've dodged a bullet, but it's important to understand the serious consequences for failing to fully perform the required service. Don't let my demeanor or the fact that you received a lesser sentence fool you. Failure to meet the sentencing requirements will lead to imposition of a harsher sentence, even jail. None of that will look good on your record."

The judge then had Zane proceed to Mrs. Natalie, the person who ran the diversion program. She gave him a choice of picking up trash, restorative justice classes, or community service at the Sara Smith center.

"I'm not picking up any trash." Zane told her.

"You have limited options here, sir," replied Mrs. Natalie.

"I'll do the Sara Smith Center."

"Great. You'll report Monday," Mrs. Natalie instructed him as she handed Zane his paperwork.

"You'll report to a guy named Justin Griffin; he's the director," she added.

"You mean Coach Justin?" Zane said, his voice trembling.

"Yep, a great guy. Good luck, Zane."

Zane had to do 40 hours of community service and pay restitution for the laptop. He was also suspended from school for a week and wasn't allowed to play in the next two football games, either. And if he didn't complete his community service, it would be much longer.

Chapter 7

Community Service

Zane reported to the Sara Smith Center on Monday.
The center was located a few blocks from his house,
but he'd never been there It was named after Sara
Smith, an astonishing lady in the community. She
was a great woman, mother, grandmother and
caretaker. She was a local hero. She helped many
families out, she always helped the youngsters out
and was an authentic beautiful leader.

The center had a huge gymnasium, an activity room
with three pool tables, a ping-pong table, and an air
hockey table. It had an art room, a computer lab, a
learning center, a library, a kitchen, and a teen
center with all the newest game systems and two
gigantic TV's. The center was for youths ages 6-18.
It provided a safe haven and was an outlet and place
to come after school. It was open Monday – Friday
from 3:00 pm to 9:00, and Saturdays from 9:00 am
to 6:00.

Coach Justin had been running the center for years, and he gave his all to it. During football season he would miss a couple hours at the center to help coach. Though, when he resigned, he was able to be back all the time again. Zane made his way to the center that Monday. It was his first day of community service, and he wasn't taking it seriously at all. He was nervous to see Coach Justin. As far as the work part, Zane assumed he would be hooping, joking, flirting with girls, and playing video games at the center all evening. Easy service hours—that was his intention.

However, he was in for a rude awakening. When he entered the center with his paperwork, he was ready to get his community service over with. He knew 40 hours was a piece of cake. He walked in the common area and saw Coach Justin hanging up posters for upcoming events.

He approached him with a huge grin and said, "What's up, Coach?"

"How are you, young man? Glad to have you here," Coach Justin replied.

"Aye, Coach. Community service is about to be a piece of cake. Just give me a basketball so I can go hoop and you can sign my paper."

"No, sir. This isn't a vacation for you," Coach Justin replied. His facial expression changed and he said in a serious tone, "Each day you'll report here. I'll have a list of things you need to do, such as clean floors and run activities."

"Man, I ain't cleaning no floors!" Zane disrespectfully replied.

"Well, then go do your community service elsewhere; go tell it to the judge."
Zane paused for a second. He had no choice; he was on his last leg. He knew he couldn't burn this bridge with Coach Justin. "Okay, Coach, you got it. Whatever you say," he replied humbly.

Coach didn't show it outwardly, but he felt deeply saddened for Zane, not the pity-type of sadness, but he felt hurt because he truly cared him.

The only reason he let Zane do his diversion and community service at the Sara Smith Center was because he wanted to help him. He knew if the courts placed him anywhere else, he'd be in trouble. Zane was a good kid at heart, but had been misinformed about the reality of life and sports since he'd been praised for his athletic ability from the time he was five years old. He lived an illusion.

Coach's plan was to give Zane lessons to inform and develop him holistically. Zane was no doubt a phenomenal athlete. He just required personal development. He often made poor decisions and he was very, very entitled.

On top of all that, he used his talents to get by; he really didn't want to work hard at all. Once again, simply misinformed about sports, opportunities and the realities of sports and life.

"I'm going to let you have today to get acclimated," Coach Justin said. They went on a tour around the center, followed by filling out paperwork. Coach showed Zane the supply closet, how to clean, the rules, expectations and regulations.

He then made a schedule of daily duties that Zane needed to complete.

"Tomorrow, meet me in the learning center. And come back in ready to work!" Coach said.

"Okay," Zane replied.

Chapter 8

Day 1: Who Are You?

"Who are you?"
"What are you good at doing?"
"What do you want to become?"

When Zane came back the following day, he clocked in and went straight to the learning room. He expected that Coach was going to make him vacuum or something. However, when he entered the room Coach Justin had three simple questions written on the board:

"Who are you?" "What are you good at?"
"What do you want to become better at?"

"Can you answer these for me, Zane"? asked Coach.

"Why are you asking these? You know who I am already," Zane replied.

Coach didn't get frustrated or mad at all. He simply told Zane, "When we meet, I really want you to listen to me and apply yourself." Zane wasn't aware, but Coach had a goal: he was going to help Zane become a better athlete by helping him becoming a better person. That was his philosophy. He believed that if you became a better person, you would be a better athlete. It was simple.

Who you are off the field, off the court and outside of the arenas had a massive effect regarding success on the field, court and arena. This applies to every athlete. More importantly, knowing who you are, what you are good at and what you want to get better at, also helps. It's about becoming more than an athlete and realizing you mean more. Coach was going to teach Zane lessons that nobody was teaching him—and it all started with "Who are you?"

"Take a few minutes, read and answer these questions for me, Zane," Coach said.
Zane read the questions in his head. Then he paused for a second, took a deep breath and answered them:

Who are you?

"Umm, I'm Zane."

What are you good at doing?

I'm good at sports—specifically, football, baseball, track and basketball.

What do you want to get better at?

"Umm… football, basketball, track, lacrosse."

Coach paused and just looked at Zane, shaking his head. He even let out an uncomfortable laugh. The answers Zane gave to Coach explained a lot. These answers showed that his entire identity was wrapped into sports, but, more importantly, it showed he had no aspirations outside of the field.

He didn't understand the balance between Clark Kent and Superman. He especially didn't understand personal branding either.

Then Coach took a turn and answered the questions:

Who are you?

"I am Justin Griffin. A father, son, brother, friend, coach, director, author, artist, mentor, teacher, speaker… and so much more."

What are you good at doing?

"I'm good at speaking, carpentry, repairing, educating, cooking, fishing, accounting, writing… and more."

What do I want to get better at?

"I want to become a better investor, a better writer, and a better mentor. I'm also working to become a better director."

"You see the difference in our answers?" Coach asked.

He paused, then continued, "Zane, you are more than just an athlete. What else are you good at? You have more to offer. Stop boxing yourself in." Coach wanted Zane to understand who he was when the helmet comes off.

Though Zane just stood there, looking confused, Coach reiterated to him, "You have to have an identity aside from sports. You've been stuck in sports and on the field of glory. But you have no clue who you are; you've lived by the expectations of others. As I always say, you have been misinformed about a lot of things. For example, why are you even here in the first place? What are you doing breaking into peoples' houses? You can't do that! But let me guess. Because you're good at sports, you feel it's okay, right?"

Coach concluded lesson time. He told Zane to go home tonight and think about "who you are when the helmet comes off."

Chapter 9

Day 2: The Real Bench

*"Don't forget: One of the saddest
things in life is wasted talent."*
Thomas Monson

When the next day dawned, Zane couldn't believe
he wasn't going to be playing in the game that week
or that he was suspended from school. He couldn't
believe that he actually had to do community
service, either. Zane arrived at the center early,
prior to it becoming packed with all the kids. Coach
met him at the door and quickly said, "Let's take a
walk." He asked the assistant director, Miss Conley,
to watch the center while he and Zane headed
outside. Zane had no clue what was going on.

"Where we going, Coach?" he asked nervously.

"Just walk." Coach had something he wanted to
show Zane, something that he really needed to see,

something that you could witness in a lot of
neighborhoods across the nation—something Zane
probably had seen numerous times but had never
really comprehended or acknowledged.
They walked about a block or two from the center,
past the apartment buildings, shopping center and
gas station. They stopped at the park.

Right in the middle of the park there was a bench
filled with a group of guys sitting there conversing
with each other. Zane glanced around and said,
"Coach, why are we out here with the bums?"

Coach was soundless for a second while he
observed the park bench.
Then he looked at Zane and said, "Bums, huh?"

"Yeah, all they do is sit out here and drink, do
drugs, fight and talk about 'coulda, woulda,
shoulda,'" said Zane.

"Nah, they aren't bums, just a couple products of
misinformation," Coach responded.

Coach took a deep breath, pointed to one of the guys at the bench, and said, "You see him?" That's Thomas from Aurora. He was one of the best quarterbacks in the nation. He had scholarship offers from everywhere. He eventually chose to play at KSU. However, he was arrested for punching a guy on campus and stealing his cash and cell phone.

Afterwards, he was kicked off the team and out of school. He just couldn't recoup after that.

Right next to him, that's Emmitt Watson. He was a hooper at Vigil T back in the day. Look him up. He once scored 72 points in a high school game. He won multiple state titles. He, too, had offers from everywhere. His banners are all over your school. Unfortunately, he didn't have the grades; he didn't apply himself.

He wasn't able to get into school anywhere. To make things worse, he got hurt. He had nothing to fall back on; he had nothing to stand on. Once he was done playing, everyone turned on him. His self-worth was in sports. Eventually, he turned to other (bad) things.

Behind him, standing in the turquoise sweater, is David Temple. He had the most potential out of everybody in that group. He was an all-star baseball player. One of the best in the nation. He was an amazing pitcher and a natural slugger. He was drafted into the major leagues fresh from high school, but he couldn't stay out of trouble. He wanted people to bow down to him and thought he was better than everyone else. He never was able to make it.

Lastly, you have Charles Jones. He was just like you—born with talent, but he lacked character and decision-making skills. He didn't want to listen to anybody and had a horrible attitude. He made poor choices, and ultimately his downfall was domestic violence—beating his girlfriend and breaking her jaw. He just could never get it right. Look at him now. Wasted talent.

Coach turned to face Zane and told him straight up that this is where he would be if he didn't change his ways. This is where he was headed—the real bench or a jail bench. "These guys were just like you, a couple of them were way better than you, as a matter of fact. All the potential in the world, but they couldn't get it together. Shoot Zane, I tried to bench you for just a game, one game, to teach you a lesson. But you didn't get it. Now, if you don't turn it around and get right, this is a bench you'll be on for life.

You'll be just like those guys, telling people what you 'coulda, woulda, shoulda did or been' and 'how good you used to be.' You don't want to be here!"

"You understand?" asked Coach Justin.
"Yes, sir," Zane humbly answered.
They went back to the center and Zane went on about his daily duties. He went home that night with a lot on his mind, but he was oblivious to Coach's message about the "real" bench that day because he felt invincible and didn't believe he could possibly be like those bums—until he searched all of them

on the internet. What he found led him to a paradigm shift. He realized Coach was telling the truth. All the people on that bench had been high-profile athletes. Coach wasn't lying—these were certified stars—who were misinformed and failed. Zane didn't want to be anything like them and bought in a little more to Coach's message and his lesson.

Chapter 10

Different Types of Athletes

Coach gave Zane a paper to study. It was a list containing the different types of athletes. He wanted Zane to study the list, then evaluate himself and select which athlete he identified with.

Mode's Athlete Identity List

- *Invincible Athlete* = The invincible athlete is an athlete that is merely focused on themselves and is so locked into sports it becomes their complete identity. They feel they can't be told anything and usually aren't coachable. The invincible athlete is someone who is misinformed on the reality of sports. This is the athlete that believes they are above the team, above the law and above rules. The invincible athlete tends to be very cocky (not to be confused with confident).

- An athlete that just doesn't listen. They are talented, smart, but their downfall is they're full of themselves.

- The invincible athlete usually always connects with other traits such as "Knucklehead Athlete" or "Abusive Athlete."

- **_Knucklehead Athlete_** = The knucklehead is an athlete that is very good at sports but can't seem to stay out of trouble. They're really talented, however, they continuously seem to be attracted to problems. You have a lot of people who are talented and fit this category. They can never make it to the next level; they can't seem to get out of their own way. Why? because they're always in trouble! The knucklehead is self-explanatory.

- **_Wasted Talent Athlete_** = Wasted talent athletes are the athletes that were really good, but didn't care about anything. Someone who has all the talent in the world, but never taps into their potential.

- They were talented and naturally athletic, but didn't want to be the star, didn't want to take advantage of opportunities.

- ***Bad grades Athlete*** = The bad grades athlete is the athlete that is dominant and really good. This athlete is very talented and even smarter than they believe they are, but they don't take school seriously. They're held back by bad grades. They can't balance school and athletics. They'll make excuses but 9/10 they don't apply themselves. They are one dimensional. Always ineligible!

- ***Abusive Athlete*** = An abusive athlete is someone who excels in sports but is abusive. They exhibit heavy violence towards women. We see these guys being kicked off their teams and in the news for domestic violence, sexual assault and worse. The abusive athlete also extends to those who abuse others in general.

- ***Overlooked Give-up Athlete*** = This is an athlete that is a decent athlete who gets overlooked, so they just give up. Lack of grit.

- ***Overlooked Thrive Athlete*** = This is someone who is overlooked but understands and continues to grind and stay tenacious and makes no excuses. They have a lot of value and are seeking to find it. They earn it and take advantage of all areas from sports, academics, and life.

- ***Partier Athlete*** = The partier athlete is blessed with the ability to play sports, but wants to do nothing but party all the time. They put partying before everything else, so they fall off, flunk out of school, end up in trouble, or just can't balance or stay focused.

- ***Social-Media Athlete*** = The Social media athlete is an athlete who lies and flexes for social media. This is an athlete that could become great but doesn't want to go through the steps it takes, so they do just enough to get social media love.

- They post misleading highlights and pictures with captions that don't match their true situation.

- The social media athlete could be very good, but they won't go through the process of what it takes and, rather, fakes it. Social media is their downfall.

- ***Well-rounded Athlete*** = The well-rounded athlete is the ultimate goal. The well-rounded athlete is informed. The well-rounded athlete understands the balance of sports and life. They take nothing for granted and work really hard.

  They use sports as a vehicle. They put in the work to be the best—from the weight room, the classroom, and even how they behave in life. Once again, well-rounded is the goal for all athletes!

  Zane looked at the list and said, "I believe I'm overlooked #2 because I should be a five-star."

  Coach shook his head, realizing Zane wasn't going to recognize his own shortcomings.

He said, "Bruh, you're a combination of Invincible and Knucklehead on your way to Wasted Talent." You fit these traits impeccably.

The ultimate goal for all athletes is to be well-rounded—meaning champions on and off the field. All-Americans on and off the court. Balanced and thriving in both life and sports, that's the end goal.

Year after year, we see the ***Invincible Athletes*** suffer from self-interference, we watch as the ***Abusive Athletes*** destroy and hurt others, we see the ***Wasted Talent Athletes*** remorse and suffer, wishing they would have applied themselves. We watch the ***Knucklehead Athletes*** collapse. We watch as the ***Partier Athletes*** ruin their opportunities and the ***Bad Grade Athletes*** miss-out. We watch how the ***Overlooked Athletes*** either give up or rise and execute. We watch the ***Social media athletes*** live in a matrix. Nonetheless, at the end of the day, the end goal that we aim for is that all athletes become ***Well-rounded athletes.***

Zane studied the list. After reading it for the eighth time, the list began to hit home. He recognized a lot of athletes he knew that fit most of the categories. For example, Samuel Jones, his friend he broke into the house with was a "Knucklehead," an amazing athlete with tons of potential but always attracted to trouble.

He also thought about his favorite professional players who went to jail. He thought about his cousin Troy Thompson, who lost a scholarship for stealing and credit card scamming.

Zane also thought about all the professional athletes he admired growing up that fit the "Abusive" category—the athletes who were great competitors but also beating women, raping women, fighting and exhibiting overall abusive behavior.

He thought about the kids who were the top in the state each year but couldn't elevate or move to the next level due to bad grades.He thought about

Lebron James and all the well-rounded athletes who were striving for greatness in sports and in life—all the athletes who took advantage of their time in competition.

Then he took a look in the mirror. He reflected on his actions in connection to the list. He knew he was far from "Well-rounded" and actually fit all the categories that any coach, team or establishment would *not* want in a player.

Chapter 11

Day 3: Character Matters

" I believe in doing the right things;
that is my
character and personality. "
-Gianluigi Buffon

Zane had been working really hard at the Sarah Smith Center. Day three came of his community service, and he was holding up fine. Coach had him mopping, scraping gum, lifting tables, and taking out trash. Zane knew that this wasn't what he wanted in life. He put in 7 hours or more a day of his required 40 hours of community service; he was on 21 hours thus far. Though Zane was exhausted from the mental and physical work, he keep pushing and buying in. Coach had Zane working the front desk while he was in his office replying to emails.

It was a quiet day; Zane was listening to music when a plumber came in to do some work on the bathrooms in the teen center. The plumber walked to the front desk and greeted Zane, "Hello, young man, I'm Morgan from Wilson Pluming. I'm here to see Mr. Justin."

With a look of disgust, Zane said, "Ehh, he's in his office. Let me grab him for you."

Coach came out his office and embraced the guy, shouting, "Mighty Mo, what's up man!!" and giving the plumber a big hug. They sat in the front and talked for a while, and when they were done, Morgan went to go work on the bathroom.

"Coach, why you so happy to talk to a damn, dusty, broke plumber?" asked Zane.

"First of all, that plumber is Morgan Wilson, former All-American receiver. He played several years in the NFL and still has tons of records from both college and professional. He ran a 4.2 forty back in the day, as well," Coach Justin explained.

"Wow, that's dope," Zane humbly replied.

"Yeah, kid, you never know who's in the room or who's around... respect everyone. Treat the janitor with the same respect as the CEO because, trust me, none of that stuff matters after you're done playing. You can't put 4.2 speed on your resume. Jobs will not care. Morgan graduated; he even has his master's in business. He started his own plumbing business and makes way more money than anyone you and I know. He's very successful. So, don't laugh at the plumber, he's working. And doing well.

Zane never thought about it like that. His entire life he was told that if you are good at sports, people will bow down to you; if you excel at sports, people will hire you anywhere/anytime—and you don't have to follow rules. He knew one of his old coaches would give him a job. Once again, he was wrong.

As the two of them sat in the front lobby area, Coach asked, "What does the phrase 'Character Matters' mean to you, Zane?"

"It means that you have to have good character to go places."

"Exactly!" shouted Coach. "A lot of athletes lack good character. So many are stuck in the box of entitlement; most have become praise junkies, and character gets put on the back burner. This is a huge part of what keeps athletes from becoming great." Athletes must always remember that your skills come second to your character. During (and well after sports are gone) your character will carry you. Character will take you places that your athletic ability won't. You have to be reachable and be teachable. You don't know everything, and when you're willing to listen and learn, you become a much better athlete and individual. Never play victim. If it's always the other person's fault—coach's fault or someone else's fault, then *you're* the problem.

You give yourself all the power to change and flourish when you take accountability for your actions.

Chapter 12

Day 4: Sacrifice "

"Follow your passion, be prepared to work hard and sacrifice, and, above all, and don't let anyone limit your dreams."
Donavan Bailey

It was very challenging and awkward for Zane, being away from his friends, teammates and the game he loved. Ironically, though, spending time with Coach, Zane was learning to respect the game. He had a realization.

He approached Coach and said, "Coach, you're right, I have been misinformed. There was so much I didn't know."

"You know what makes the great players great?" replied Coach Justin.

"Practice and behaving?" Zane responded.

"Doing the little things right, and, more importantly... sacrifice.

Each year thousands of sports organizations, schools, teams, clubs and coaches lose some of their best athletes and recruits due to the dumbest occurrences. Yet it all comes down to learning how to sacrifice. This is an area where tons of athletes have been misled because they aren't taught how to sacrifice. We have to learn—and it starts early. We must teach our athletes early about sacrifice. That's one of the biggest keys to success. It's easy to get in trouble; it's easy to go to that party and turn up. It's easy to go to the mall and fight, and it's easy to rob people. It's easy to do the wrong thing.

The best athletes make sacrifices. They go home early, they sacrifice party time, they sacrifice the turning up because they know the sacrifice will pay off. You have to learn how to sacrifice, Zane. Sacrifice who you are for who you want to become. Due to the fact athletes are different from those who don't participate in athletics, we have expectations, not goals.

We are expected to behave, be role models and carry ourselves with dignity. We are expected to work hard, produce and be great."

Take Nothing for Granted

If you chose not to buy in and be a team player, the name of the game is burn and turn. It's the truth. Sports don't last forever. Coaches are always recruiting to replace you or find someone better. "You are hired to be fired," Coach Justin said. It's a business. However, many aren't informed about this. They believe that they can chill, relax, and not work hard. Most athletes believe they have time. The truth is you *don't* have time. You only have the *now* so take advantage.

This is why I have "Take nothing for granted on the board."

- **You don't have time! But everyone thinks they have time.**

- **Stay consistent, stay working out. Study and master your craft.**

- **Enjoy every moment. When you're done, you're done.**

- **You have to maximize every opportunity**.

Zane understood everything Coach was talking about. He thought about all the things he took for granted. His sophomore football season was coming to an end, and he was going to miss two games. To make things even more interesting, he received a text from a friend that said, "What's up, bro. CU coaches came to visit the school but you were nowhere to be found." Zane was hurt that his own actions led him to miss an opportunity with his dream school.

Social Media

One of the biggest reasons that athletes are misinformed today is social media. Social media can be an amazing tool and has tons of benefits. However, for many young athletes, social media has them very misinformed. Misinformed on how things really work, misinformed on what goes into being great and misinformed on hard work.

"They live vicariously through their idols in professional sports and routinely only see the glamorous side of that life. Private jets, endorsement deals, big houses, etc. They don't see the work that is put in behind the scenes. Many students do not understand the work that it takes to be a special player at the high school level and then how exponentially harder it is to be a unique talent on the collegiate level. Fair or not, I think like many of their peers in music, entrepreneurship, or other specialized fields – many young athletes have people who support them that constantly tell them they are the best at what they do and they deserve the best. Self-awareness is not something that is often talked about and that needs to change" - *Wesley Mass Assistant Vice President, SAAC, Florida International University*

Coach told Zane that social media is to be used responsibly. Zane was highly influenced by social media. He felt because he had thousands of followers and constantly had people worshipping him that he was untouchable. He saw his favorite athletes living it up and he emulated that, not understanding what they did to get there. Zane truly didn't understand what it took to be a special player. Coach made him aware of how important sacrifice and self-awareness is to student athletes.

Anger

"Coach, what happened to you playing professionally?" asked Zane

Coach was a former Running back. He played football at the University of Colorado. He was a hard worker and a tenacious athlete.

"My journey was interesting" Coach replied. "I broke my ankle my senior year of college, the Kansas City Chiefs were going to sign me following the draft that year however my ankle was still in recovery mode. When it finally got rehabilitated, I reached out but they had moved on. So, I went to play Arena Football. I dominated in the arena league" Coach Justin explained.

"Well what happened…then what?" Zane asked
"I let my anger get in the way of my ambitions" Coach replied.

As athletes we play with a lot of emotion. Nobody likes to lose. One emotion that we see a lot in sports is anger. It's okay to be angry however you can't let the anger affect your success…

"I was playing a big game and I got into a fight with the other team. This wasn't a regular fight; I went off on the players, coaches and refs. I got ejected" coach explained

Zane sat in shocked while hearing this from Coach.

"My coach came to me after the game with tears in his eyes and said the Chargers were in the stands and wanted to sign me but after seeing my character, they wanted nothing to do with me."

"OMG" said Zane

"Yea, like I said its okay to be angry we all get angry but when the anger affects your success it's a problem." Coach repeated

Coaches don't want to deal with or invest in guys with bad character or behavioral issues like I displayed. I was out of character and it cost me. That's why I want to help you. said Coach

Chapter 13

Day 5: Academics & Athletics
"Good athletes with bad grades become hometown legends that never got out of their hometowns.
That's not a fraternity you want to join."
-Derek Jones

Coach was checking up on Zane in regards to his school progress. Due to the fact that Zane was suspended, Coach wanted to make sure he didn't fall behind in school. But Zane was already behind. Coach found out that Zane was failing several classes and also discovered that the coaches at the school were mysteriously making Zane eligible anyway. Coach Justin needed to help Zane out for long-term success—graduation, academics, schooling and beyond.

Coach recognized that as soon as something happened, or if Zane wasn't able to return, they'd ultimately move on to the next person. Zane would be left on his own.

The name of the game is burn and turn. Which is why he needed to take advantage of every opportunity. Athletes need to really understand that. You are not just an athlete. You're a *student* athlete. Student comes first. Athletes all over the nation have been misinformed for years with the idea that you have to focus only on one thing (sports).

They've been misinformed on the importance of balancing student obligations and the athletic regime. You can't get to the pros without college being an option. You can't get to college if you aren't playing. You can't play if you don't have the grades. Sports can open doors, so take advantage! Take school seriously you won't have sports forever.

Reed Clifton Story

Coach asked Zane if he knew who Reed Clifton was. Zane replied, "No, sir." Zane had never heard of Reed; neither had a lot of people.

"Reed was the man," said Coach.

"Coach, not another one of your athletes who fell off stories," protested Zane.

"This story is unique," Coach explained. "Reed was a beast ever since he was in middle school. He excelled at basketball from a very young age. He actually excelled in other high school sports too, winning multiple championships. He went on to play at USC. During his freshmen year in college, though, he got into a bad accident and was never able to play basketball again.

He proved himself in the game of basketball and then something bad happened. However, Reed returned to his middle school about year after that."

"Was he a Principle? Teacher? Gym teacher? Restorative justice person?" asked Zane.

"No, he was a student," Coach replied.

Zane stood silent.

"Reed didn't have any education. People were passing him because of social promotion and his incredible basketball skills. Truth was, he could barely read; he literally was at a sixth grade level in all academic standings. He had to return to middle school and take night classes."

Chapter 14

Chalk Talk: Visions vs. Hallucinations

Coach had "V" and "H" written on the board. The
V = Vision and the H = Hallucination.

"Zane, what's the difference between vision and
hallucination?"

"Umm, a vision can be manifested. It's something
you can see and work towards. A hallucination is
something that doesn't exist at all, like make-
believe. You're seeing things," Zane replied.

"Correct!" replied Coach. Then he asked Zane to
name a long-term goal, a short-term goal, and three
colleges he wanted to attend.

Zane replied, my long-term goal is to go to college;
my short-term goal is to win state this year in
football, basketball and lacrosse.

My colleges I want to attend are the University of Colorado, the University of Kansas, and Florida International.

"Ask yourself, are these Visions or Hallucinations? Coach responded.
"Do your habits match these goals? Can they be manifested?"

"Right now, they're hallucinations," mumbled Zane.
"How are you going to win state if you can't play? How are you going to go to college if you stay in trouble? Think about it!" Coach pushed. "You're capable, but are you willing? You got to be willing to make that vision come true. You have to bring it to life!

Message to the Reader

Are your goals visions or hallucinations?

Are your habits matching your actions?

Are you manifesting—or just seeing things?

<u>Chalk Talk: Make Life Your Sport</u>

Are you an athlete?

Do you want to win championships?

Do you want to go to college?

Do you want a full ride scholarship?

Do you want to play professional?

The answer to all these questions above should be
"YES!"

There are a lot of ways that sports and sports
competition can positively drive and impact one's
life. Once again, nothing wrong with playing a sport
and being a driven athlete. There's nothing negative

about playing a sport. Sports are very beneficial. Playing sports aids in physical development, good health, and helps develop a necessary life skill, teamwork. Sports were made for recreational purposes. However, overtime sports and the role they play in society have evolved into almost an obsession. Especially when it comes to true prospects. No matter how great you become, no matter where you are, don't ever forget to make *life* your sport.

Chapter 15

Day 6: Support & Redemption

Finally, Zane was on his last day of community service. He had done a pretty good job, and Coach was satisfied with how he had risen to every occasion. Coach had a meeting with Zane's mother Laura before signing him off. He knew it was important to talk to her, and that she was a key component to Zane's development. Every parent thinks their child is the next LeBron James or Odell Beckham, Jr. and so on.

But we have to stop putting high expectations on our kids to be someone they're not and, instead, push them to be their own person. Coach Justin looked at Zane's mom and said, "Laura, you have the power to change and mold your child's life. I need you to do that."

"I understand," she replied.

"Also, stop living through the kid vicariously. Living vicariously through your kid is one of the worst things you can do. Just let him play!" Coach urged her.

"You're right. I just thank you for helping us."

We are missing out on being able to be well rounded because of fundamental over-valuation. We are missing out on proper valuation of learning. We devalue the thing that helps create true value all because we can dunk, or we run this time or can make a jumper. Very few kids see success outside of athletics.

We are also miseducated around the longevity of sports. Sports is not the reality. The reality is numbers don't lie. Look at history. Not everyone is going to go pro. But you can make life your sport. We are missing out on being able to learn, and even help our communities, because we are misinformed.

Many athletes grow up without a keen understanding of life's possibilities. They don't understand the system. They think it's one thing and eventually realize it's something else.

It's sad to watch athletes think they are doing something valuable and then realize they were being used and never truly valued as a human being to begin with. This can leave someone mentally unstable. Once they can no longer perform at a high level, they are tossed out, and it's on to the next one. All parents need to push their children to be better people and better athletes, but they need to understand this dynamic—and help their kids understand it.

"It's time to grow," Zane said quietly to himself. Community service had come to an end and Zane was free to leave. He had all his hours signed off on and he was clear.

Coach had one last message for him, and it was, "No matter how fast you are you'll never out run the justice system, stay focused!" coach continued on "Follow through. You have to follow through, apply everything you've learned, learn from the lessons you were taught, and learn how to take criticism."

Zane shook his head and said, "Yes, sir, it's time to grow."

Coach and Zane shook hands as Zane was exiting the building. "Thank you for helping me, Coach." Coach took out an envelope and gave it to Zane, "I just want you to be the great Mr. Zane Thompson."

Zane opened the envelope and it was the money Zane owed for the laptop he stole. "Thank you, Coach!"

"Now, Zane, I want you to know your story is going to be big. You're going to impact the world. We make mistakes but we rise. Just make sure you pass these lessons on and help someone else. Lead by example. It's not always going to be perfect, but do your best to improve daily in all areas.

A lot of people have watched you grow, all eyes on you. Set the example."

"I will, Coach, and thanks for all your help," replied Zane.

Zane returned to school. The first clear sign that he was going to do things differently was his being early to class and sitting in the front row. He was ready to focus. Though he wasn't able to play in the upcoming game, he knew that he had to stay on point and take care of things the right way.

The following week Zane continued to stay focused. His behavior was totally different. That didn't mean he wasn't experiencing challenges. He just had a different mindset from where he was before to now. He returned to practice ready to compete. The team had lost one game in his absence; Zane was ready to help the team.

Game day came. It was a cool, brisk evening at the Falcon's stadium. The Virgil T. High school Falcons were playing against the East Aurora Raiders. It was Zane's first game back. He was ready to make an impact. However, this time it meant much more. He was still the dominate phenom and had that natural ability, except now he was even more of a threat since he was in a better head space.

Zane had stepped out of that mindset of misinformation. He had become knowledgeable about the true value of sports and athletics. He devoted himself to becoming well-rounded. Coach Justin had returned to coaching and was now teaching classes to his fellow coaches on the misinformation of athletes and how having amazing athletes with even better character can win titles.

Zane decided to walk into his greatness… and you can too!

Zane's Letter

I want to thank you, Coach. Nobody had ever shown me the importance of Student Athlete Enrichment. As athletes, we've always been encouraged daily to only become a better player. We never really learned how to be better people. Winning often gets put before character. We have expectations put on us, instead of learning them for ourselves. Our parents only care about our athletic success, and everything else is neglected. You helped me realize the Golden Secret when it comes to sports and athletics.

The Golden Secret is that you won't become a better person by being a better athlete, but you will become a better athlete by being a better person. I hid behind my athleticism because I didn't want to push myself in life, so I only relied on my athletic ability.

You helped me break out of the cages I was trapped in. I had become so good and so popular because of my athletic ability that I thought I was indestructible. I thought I was above the law. I thought I was in invincible and that rules, school, directions, and systems didn't apply to me. They say "ball is life," but what happens when you can't ball anymore?

To the Athletes

I wrote this book for all the athletes in the world. No matter where you come from or what you play, athletes need personal development. My purpose, motivation and the goal of this book is to help athletes understand the importance of becoming well-rounded. There are so many amazing programs out there that train athletes and educate them on how to get better, but ultimately, they are being trained to develop their athleticism, not necessarily their character. Athletes need life skills. Athletes need to understand consequences. Athletes need personal enrichment. Athletes need to learn the truth about sports. The name of the game is "burn and turn." You don't know it at first, but your sport, coaches, school, team, and others will burn you and turn you. This means that they will use you and get rid of you. This sounds bad, but it's the game. On the flip side, you have to "get yours," meaning if you're in this position, take advantage of every opportunity (interdependence). I understand it takes a village; thus, I went and asked some friends and family to contribute guidance in the "Pro Huddle".

Pro Huddle

"Character is what matters the most... the best athletes usually aren't the most talented. They usually have the best character which includes work ethic, accountability, honor, and mental/physical toughness."- *Cornelius Lucas, OL, Chicago Bears*

"Everyone gets put back down to reality, and no matter what, you will be humbled at some point. Character matters." - *Phillip Lindsay, RB, Denver Broncos,*

"Look up all the athletes that 'almost' made it. But missed the grades or got in trouble. Don't be like them, take care of business" - *Kalen Ballage, RB, Miami Dolphins*

Character will lead to better grades. Take pride in being the best. The best isn't one dimensional." - *Christian McCaffrey RB, Carolina Panthers*

"Character is how legends are made. If you want to just be basic and not take pride in character, you won't get too far." - *Jamillah Lang, University of Colorado, Women's Basketball Legend, professional athlete and Hall of Fame inductee*

"School and athletics go hand and hand, so view school as the key to success because athletics won't last forever. No matter how many records you set or championships you've won! That degree or diploma you get from walking across that stage will open up doors that athletics won't take you to. Your character will reflect your family, school and program. Just know there are many eyes watching you automatically because you are an athlete. People are looking up to you no matter what." - *Samaj Johnson. TE Washburn University*

"Coaches won't even look at you if you can't take care of business, and with a bad attitude, you'll just be another person decent at sports playing semi-pro. School and character make you golden as an athlete." - *Keontae Edwards, DB, Black Hills University*

"Your talent may open doors for you but your work ethic and character are what actually secure the job. Scouts come and talk to academic advisors about prospects nonstop and they want to know about that individuals' character. This industry is a business, nobody is going to invest billions into an individual who could potentially embarrass their entire organization. The LeBron's and Kobe's of the world are rare. Most athletes are going back and finishing their degrees behind the screens during the off season because they realize the importance of education and having a degree". *-Ashley Cruder, Auburn University, Track and Field*

"Look at every athlete that has had their draft stock dropped, been suspended. Banned from the league because they had the entitlement and character issues. Look at all the hood legends that didn't take school seriously, so every conversation with them is what could-of, would-of, should-of happened if they got their grades right." *- Zavier Steward, RB, Mississippi Valley College, Professional RB*

"Look up character in the dictionary and look up a story of a young athlete who never had a chance because of his character—and didn't get a chance. So many stories out there, don't let it be you. Be great!" - *Chris Young, SS, Denver Broncos, Georgia Tech Alum*

"If you stay on the wrong path, you'll be out of sports quick. The game isn't long to begin with so not giving 100% to everything that benefits you such as school, taking care of your body, workouts is going to be hard to overcome. Don't be afraid to be great.:" *Brett Hundley, QB Arizona Cardinals*

"I grew up with multiple guys that were even more talented than me but never got the chance to show that potential pass pop warner because they were never eligible in high school. A lot of good athletes fall off because sports come easy to them. So when they get to a point in life where they have to work for things, they don't know how to respond because they never prepared for the situation." - *Robbie Rouse, NFL Running Back, Fresno State all- time Rushing Leader*

"I've seen thousands of athletes fall off…literally seen the most successful people in sport become nothing because they allowed a 5-second decision to ruin their lives. Some were 5-star recruits, Heisman watch list type of guys, projected first-rounder's, but they either smoked away their opportunity or failed out of school by not giving their academic effort. Talent will only take you so far, but character will keep you there. Character is not only doing the right thing when someone is watching; that's called being a Hollywood actor.

"Character is doing the right thing over and over and over again when no one is watching because it is the right thing to do. These young men and women who fell off only did the right thing when they received accolades or were in the spotlight, but at the times when it really counted to have character, they had none, so their talent took them somewhere that their character couldn't keep them."

- *Chase Moore DB, University of Texas*

"Character is one of the most important things and sports also helps build character. You face so many obstacles when playing sports. It tests you as an individual and you find out who you really are. Are you someone who gets through adversity? Someone who folds? Do you have heart? Are you a leader? Character is everything on and off the field. You have to find out what type of teammate you want to be and person. Sports puts that all on the front line. I knew some girls at my juco that had the ability to go D1 but didn't because they weren't on top of their grades and they missed their opportunity. Then I've also seen athletes that just had bad attitudes and were kicked off of teams but were really good but just couldn't buy in to the team. It doesn't matter how good you are if you can't get accepted into the big-time schools because of your grades. There is ALWAYS somebody else out there just as good or better. So talented as you may be. If you can't lead and be a good teammate and or pass classes, they'll pass on you and you'll end up taking the hard route. If you want to be special. Be that talented AND come with everything else, that's special. That's what is going to make you different then everybody else. A lot of people can hoop not everybody has the character to be great"-*Shae Kelley, WNBA, University of Minnesota Alum.*

"What happens in one aspect of your life is bound to happen in another. If you're not taking care of business in the classroom, how are you going to take care of business on the field/court? If you aren't a person of high character and integrity off the field, how do you expect your teammates to count on you when things get hard on the field. You can't just be a good athlete and expect everything to fall in line 'cause it's not; you got to put the work in in all aspects of life. I've seen first-hand, dudes with NFL talent not be able to get on the field cause they only wanna ball and not do nothing else. If that's your attitude, your whole life if going to be off balance." - *Josiah Hall, University of Wyoming, DE*

"I've played with guys better than me on the field, and going into the pros, they got zero opportunities. Meanwhile, I've had dozens of opportunities. At the end of the day, your coaches play a huge part in your transitioning to the pros or even college. Coaches and recruiters are going to ask what type of person you are. Talent can take you only so far. There are countless athletes we've seen get written off because of a bad attitude. Don't be the person to regret their actions years down the line because of a bad attitude." *- Derrick Morgan, DB, UTEP/Stony Brook /Professional Athlete*

"If sports were taken away, would people look at you the same? Sports opens a lot of doors if you're a good person, but only being an athlete restricts your opportunity for growth." - *Palmer White, OL /Atlanta Falcons*

"Sports are going to use you, and no matter who you are...sports end. What doesn't end is who you are and what you did. That goes with you all the way until death. So, if you think character doesn't matter, then you're saying that half your life doesn't matter. You're saying that your life is summed up by that 2.3-year average that people play in the league. Who you are is more important than what you do. Be a great man first." - *Jordan Murphy, Body by Murph; University of Colorado, FB*

"I would tell young athletes about the importance of humility. What's taken for granted will be taken away. Also a degree should always be top priority. My story is a good example. I tore my Achilles at my pro day and couldn't go to the NFL." - *Larry Butler, LB, New Mexico State*

"Don't worry about nothing but working hard... have to be focused and out-work everyone! Stay away from distractions!" - *Jaleel Awini, Air Force QB, University of Colorado, LB*

"There is a limit to how far you can go without school no matter how talented." - *Sam Jones, OL, Arizona Cardinals*

"Make plays and make grades! Never be complacent with getting better. Learn to play the game to dominate, not compete."
 - *Terrance Surratt, DL, University of South Carolina*

"Can't teach effort. Effort can flourish when you're decent. Doesn't matter what school you go to, just shine when your name is called." - *Malcolm Creer, RB, University of Colorado*

"Get rid of that entitlement! People don't care about you being good. Good doesn't put you ahead of the person with decent grades, and good character just needs a little fine tuning. Coaches don't care that you're talented because they have images to maintain on their roster and a salary to keep. College sports is a business just like the league. Bad grades and bad character will land you on ya mom's couch quicker than you can say I." - *Shavonne White, University of Vermont WBB*

"Check yourself at the door every day! Understand your role for the team and classroom. There's always a purpose with what you're doing." - *Jonathan Brown, CSU, Pueblo, Colorado*

"Focus on what's important right now (school, sports) because bad choices can affect your future. Focus on getting a scholarship and making the right choices". - *Alexis Jean, Virginia Tech WBB*

"People don't care that you play sports because, just like you, someone else is just as good or better. Your character, your grind and what can you stand on longer—a book or a football? I think that translates to life. Like you can't play football forever. You must appreciate the game to get what you want out of it, but without school you won't get far. And if you don't have character, you really won't play at a high-level cause everything isn't sweet on the next level everyone is as good as you. Everyone was all-state wherever they are from, so what's gonna separate you from the others competing for that starting spot? Your character, your grit, your passion!" - *Métise Moore, TE, Alcorn State/ Towson football*

"Humble pie is often served when we least expect it. It's all good until it's not all good. Do the right things now so you don't look like a fool later." - *Tevin Hood, University of California, Assistant Coach*

"Discipline is something to hold at a high regard because that's what propels us to them dreams." - *Caleb Madden, Alabama State*

"Don't take life for granted. Live your life, your dream, and nobody else's. Embrace the adversity that comes with it because that adversity is going to allow you to grow and make a successful outcome."

- Tevin Davis, DT, Valdosta State

"When I was being recruited that they searched my social media and some girls that I played with in high school missed out on potential scholarships because of how they carried themselves in person and on social media. Also, I think school is extremely important. You still need test scores and grades to get into a college. Also, God forbid anything happens that doesn't allow you to play sports anymore; you need to be able to have a degree to fall back on at the very least. I feel like both of those things are extremely important prior to college, in college, and especially life after collegiate athletics. Character is everything."

- Courtney Dudley, Soccer, University of Houston

"You're an injury away from not ever physically playing again. Your mind will take you further in life because you'll be a former player longer than a current player. You can't build a kingdom without a solid foundation." *- Daniel Munyer, OL*

Indianapolis Colts

"Your current level is as high as you're going to go. Even if you have offers, they are not committable offers because you have no grades to qualify. Then in a year or two, you will be forgotten because you didn't take advantage of opportunity. And opportunity doesn't get missed... it just is given to someone else." - *Coach Tre Watson, Defensive Backs Coach, University of Oregon*

"Look at the requirements needed to get into a D1 school institution and measure where you at to where you need to be. Think about local guys that you may know or have heard about that didn't make it out because they couldn't stay eligible, focused or made poor decisions. Sometimes when you're so hard-headed, it's almost best that you don't make it right away because it humbles you. Then when you hit the Juco route, you become hungrier and wiser than before. It's not the most ideal way, it's tough, but if you can't get it corrected before getting to that point, then that's the best option." - *Chidera Uzo Dribe, University of Kansas Assistant Coach, University of Colorado Alum, New Orleans Saints DE*

"To be honest, The NFL stands for... not 'national football league'... but NOT FOR LONG. The league doesn't need you. They have millions of guys wanting to get there. Character is important because it's tested through adversity. When you're not solid, you're going to fold. It is a team game! In order to get to the NFL, you have to go to college. It's no pass no play rule. There are so many good athletes that never make it and never get to experience the life... because they are too selfish to understand that they must do their part".

"Kids don't understand how important education is until it's too late. Some of the best athletes are in prison.... no one will ever know how good they are. It's all about choices. Got to make the choice to take care of your business in order to get to the level that you want to be on." - *Cyrus Gray, NFL Running Back, Texas A&M legend,*

"Building a relationship and connections are the most important things you could ever do, and when all fails, all you can do is rely on your relationship that you have made with people—and sometimes just having good character can get you in the door anyway." - *Dwayne Wallace, OL, University of Kansas*

"Life is about choices. With a piece of paper, write down one side 'fighting, drinking, sex, jail, failure.' The other side, write 'degree, parents proud, the people that you are with proud, and get paid because of what you will learn along the way.' So, you got good choices and you got bad choices. It's a definite that your bad choices will lead you down the wrong road. Give yourself a chance by making good choices. - *Jamil Merrill, DL, Rutgers University, Chicago Bears*

"There is no ball without school. If you want to continue playing, you need the grades to go to college. Without college, there is no means to an end of becoming a great player and getting a paycheck to play the game. - *Tim Lucas, Professional, WR, University of Illinois*

"Some kids think just because they're naturally talented that they don't have to put in the work. That's only half the battle. Athleticism is more than just physical—it's mental, emotional and spiritual. Your perception of how you see yourself determines how far you'll get. Which is why having a good attitude with a great work ethic always out-does someone with natural abilities and a piss poor attitude." - *Toni Smith, Oklahoma Track and Field*

"I would say character is everything! College coaches not only want a good player but someone who is a good person in and off the field. It's important to quit those bad behaviors now before it's too late. As for grades you need good grades period if you don't have the grades you don't play and there's no exceptions"-*Qiana Barfield, Adams State University, Lacrosse*

"Look at all the athletes now and compare them to the 90s and research them. You have to have decent character now to have longevity in a sport and with media, they are cracking down on everything because now everything is visible." – *Leabre McNeal, Clark Atlanta Alum*

Stay in school. Sports can only be there for so long. Once that's gone, what do you have to fall back on? Education is everything and at the end of it all, your education is a lifetime.... sports aren't." - *Donnie Mc Elroy, Mile High Blaze Head Coach*

"Talent and character will go hand in hand at the next level since everybody is either just as good/better than you. Your character and how you carry yourself outside of sports will give you a slight edge when it comes to playing time and your coaches wanting you to be a part of what they got going on. Same with teachers when it comes to the little things. But yeah, as unfortunate as it is, that's one of those situations where guys gotta learn for themselves. You can talk and advise them all you want, but it'll be on them when it's all said and done. Ball don't last forever, and having that degree or even GED will go a long way. But yeah, that's just something that comes with maturity. "Biggest thing is knowing you need the grades to even be considered for an offer/scholarship. The talent won't mean anything if, because of your grades, you aren't able to continue doing what you feel like you're best at. It's like ball is the car and the grades are the gas. At some point if you're only relying on one of the two, you gone be stuck." - *Tre O'Neal, Basketball Nichols State*

"In order to succeed you need to study the game. To be able to study the game you need to know how to learn. Talent will get you the door, the ability to be coached and learn keeps you on the roster. I've seen many athletes fall. Sometimes it was attitude/friction with coaches, others it was pure talent but lack of discipline. The high school years are the hardest - your body/ability finally catches up to the mental aspect you have drilled into you since you were a kid, but if you don't have the right player/coach dynamic or even something as seemingly disconnected as a player who has issues at home it would stop progress and potential. When I was still a kid, I had a coach give the cliché line of *being an athlete does not create character, it reveals it.* At the time I had no idea how to wrap my head around it but now it makes complete sense. No one is going to open doors for you, nothing is going to be handed to you. Your job, as an athlete, is to lean into what skills you have and cultivate it in whatever way(s) you are able - on and off the ice (, field/course).When my grades dropped because I was careless, I saw that as losing my chance to leave my town, some didn't care and figured their talent would save them. Those people are STILL in my small town lol Nowadays I feel like athletes, in general, lack the authenticity and character required for the hard work. Yes, it is a generalization and I own that, but I feel like so many people aren't willing to dig in and do the work"-*Kat Vierzba, Women's Golf/ Women's Hockey, University of Colorado*

"One thing that school teaches you is how vital discipline is to success. You are going to need that every step of the way, just because you do not want to do work doesn't mean it's not in your best benefit moving forward. There will be things in life you don't want to do, like schoolwork, but that discipline you have, will in turn, get you the grades that you need to then go off and live out your dreams in the future. Discipline prepares you for the future, not for the present, and your dreams take time to manifest. As for character, it means everything. From a sports standpoint, coaches will choose a good overall man with great character before they choose a man that is only good at sports. I first-hand have seen that you are never too good; your spot can always be replaced, regardless of who you are. Being a high character guy can move you further ahead in sports than just being good; it takes more than just talent. "The moment you feel like you are above everyone and everything, is the moment the world and this business will show you that you aren't. Stay even keeled and let your character bring you your successes." *- Carlton Hurst, University of South Dakota, Professional Basketball Player*

Character isn't a trait or just your reputation for what you can do on the field; it's the ultimate measure of who you are as a young man/woman above and greater than the "game" we play. If you're good at sports and you set a school record, someone can and will always break that record, and your record could be forgotten. The values or "code" that you live is what your character is made up of. What would you want to be remembered for? Remember, records can be broken. It's all about impact. Also, neglecting school nowadays as an athlete will guarantee you shoot yourself in the foot. Education is paired with sports; they go hand, no way around it. I challenge young athletes to be real with themselves and not be fake and only go hard on the field. Go hard in everything you do because that is what makes you a good athlete—being well rounded. No great player ever was one-dimensional; all were good in every aspect—defense, offense, and specialized—in one of those to top it off." - *Daniel Masfolo, University of Hawaii*

"Be coachable, make good choices off the field. Move forward and be relentless towards the goal.... always set hold short n long term it'll help you progress and it's results I can see." - *LJ Strollman*, Professional DB

Whatever dreams you think you're going to have won't happen if your character is bad. Committing to school and doing sports at the same time shows character and so many positive traits as a human and an athlete which is what people/coaches like and that is exactly what coaches at the next level look for... Commitment and responsibility and to be able to trust their players. Players that don't go through school and commit shows poor character and coaches refuse to deal with that nonsense because the player has become a liability and someone, they cannot trust which regardless of the talent they will drop the best player without question- *Jordan Post, Midfielder, Metro State University.*

You can't do anything without school. You have to look at school as job. You have to be on time, follow directions, getting tasks done, being respectful to others and if you can't do that you mess your money up. Same thing with school. If you can't do these things you mess your grades up which means you can't play and do the one thing you truly want to do. School is also like your security blanket. God forbid you get hurt but it happens every day. You'll have something to fall back on instead of working at McDonald's the rest of your life because you thought school wasn't important. Now you have to go back to school and be in debt because you didn't want to handle business. There's a consequence for every action you do. It your choice to make the result good or bad- *Terrell Thompson, Linebacker, Utah State*

"The game respects those who work hard and respect the grind. Partying and fighting are part of life, but that can't control you. If you love the game enough, you must give up the nonsense and focus on what is most important to. You can't have both. Partying and fighting do not mix with the game. It's not an easy fix, but you gotta put your all into what's important, one day at a time.

"As far as school goes, you won't go far without an education. Sure, you could get drafted from a junior college, but you've also got to be a top 10 prospect. The best way to get exposure is to go to a D1. The way you get into a D1 is good grades. There's no difference between talent at that level. It boils down to who works the hardest on and off the field. The key to going far is to getting into a good school that has avenues into the pros. Most D1 guys get drafted; most don't go to the show, but a lot of them will be part of an organization. Grades mix with ball. It's the best way to go the farthest. That, and staying healthy; partying and fighting won't allow you to stay healthy. - *Anthony Wilson, Adams State Baseball, Professional Baseball Player*

"One of the best lessons I have learned in my career, both personally as a student-athlete and as an administrator – our career as an athlete will end. It always does. Whether by our choice and old age, an injury, the lack of opportunity to continue playing, or at the point where we cannot continue to be competitive at a high level. For many athletes, even if they are blessed to have an experience as a professional athlete, this still puts an end to their 'identity as an athlete' around their 30's. With today's accomplishments in nutrition, fitness and the medical field, more and more people are living until their late 80's, if not to their 100's. That means that when your identity as an athlete ends, you still have 60-70 years left on this earth. My question is, what do you want to do at that point to be happy over those years? Take advantage of the opportunities that athletics provides you. At the collegiate level, use your scholarship and exposure to build your brand and get an education in an area that you feel can provide you a career when your athlete identity ends. Especially collegiate athletes, you are on a campus with thousands of talented students in their specialized field. Marketing,

Media, Entrepreneurs, people that you could connect with now and build relationships with that might be able to help you in your life after athletics. Take your headphones off and say hello to that student sitting next to you. Take 10 minutes to research the faculty on your campus on LinkedIn. How might they help you this year, 5 years from now, 20 years from now, based on their experiences? Build a network while you have leverage and cultivate it over time. Take the time to find out what will bring you happiness. What can you see yourself doing over the next 60 years?"

- Wesley Mass, Vice President/ Director Florida International University

"So, what I believe about character... there are three different people in this world and that also live in our heart. Wise, foolish, and bad. I believe you find out about someone's character when the truth comes (not when bad things happen, bad things pull bad things out) but you find out when the truth comes. The truth is the light (reality). When truth comes to a wise person, they will thank you for the feedback and the truth. They won't adjust the truth or reality.

When the foolish person receives the light/reality/truth in feedback, they will adjust it. They will dim the light, shift it, adjust it etc. The foolish is probably the smartest because they can manipulate reality. They will leave the problem outside of the room. Lack of taking responsibility. The bad person is destructive. They will bring a person down and the people in the situation. Now I believe we have all of these in us. Feedback/truth will grow your character. Feedback/truth isn't a comfortable thing to always hear. With sports, performance and results don't define your character. Pursuing integrity does. Integrity means whole. Wholeness. To be a whole athlete is not just the physical qualities. We put a lot of pressure on the physical qualities of your game but what about the mind and spirit? When we collectively pursue integrity/wholeness in all of these, then we will be a whole athlete.

Academics, training, studying school, the game, being a good student, a good son, a good brother/sister, a good friend, etc. is pursuing wholeness. Let's take the classroom from the wise, foolish, and bad personal. Each person receives a grade C on a paper. The wise person receiving their paper would accept my grade and the feedback and would look at the mistakes to work for a better grade next time. The foolish person would blame the teachers grading, or say they had practice, work etc or other excuse which is most likely valid but can't accept the grade and blame everyone else. The foolish person will try and ruin the class. I'm going to bring this classroom down, the teacher down, etc. and add excuses. Success is a bad teacher. Live in reality and be able to receive feedback". *-Tommy Flanagan Director of Strength 2Strength Performance, University of Nebraska-Kearney Football Alum*

"First and foremost, the biggest thing to me is helping these young athletes understand that their skill set in sports will only go as far as the other skill sets, they possess as young men and women. So, lacking character, discipline, integrity, and resilience shows up on the football field and beyond. Being 'decent' isn't enough, and part of the reason they are only decent is because they haven't trained all of their tools. Athletes know that we are only as good as our weakest attribute because when adversity hits, that attribute will be tested. Not having focus and discipline truly will show up in the 4th quarter. So, the main piece for me would be to illustrate that weakness in those areas will leave you at decent at best. Secondly, although obvious, it's essential to illustrate how finite football really is AND along with that, the advantage we have as athletes beyond the field.

The first part is crucial to understand. In a lifetime, football is microscopic in terms of playing. So being limited to just football, hinders advancement in other areas. Having a multitude of skill sets allows us to go beyond the field and truly be set for life. The second part to that is key for me personally, because I feel that we as coaches and mentors need to illustrate how the tools we gain through sports translate into life, figuratively—but most importantly, literally. Companies hire former athletes for a reason. Most kids take that copout route because they lack the confidence that they have in football for other areas and don't see how empowered they really are. Football players understand the process of faith and patience without even knowing it. We set to be better by 'next season,' which is months and months away. Therefore, short-term and long-term goals are something we have down pat. And that's just one component of sports that we have as a skill set. So, my final piece would illustrate to a young athlete is that he is more powerful than he truly knows and that he is only hindering himself by being shortsighted." - *Aaron Aiken, QB, Georgetown University/Coastal Carolina/Professional Quarterback*

About the Author

Popularly known as "Mode," Josh Ford is an author of athlete-development books, self-help, non-fiction, autobiographies and children's books. Prior to picking up his pen, he made a name for himself as a pro-athlete and was renowned for his enthusiasm and diligence. When Josh saw many new and aspiring athletes going down the wrong path, he got his writing career in gear, taking on the social responsibility of putting every athlete on track. Although he has transitioned as an athlete, he remains a pioneer of athlete enrichment, working alongside athletes such as Phil Lindsay, Christian McCaffery, Kalen Ballage, and Brett Hundley, amongst other top-rated athletes.

Bringing his philanthropy to the surface, Josh delights in mentoring and empowering young people. Thus, he connects with youths by sharing inspirational stories, speaking at conferences and authoring results-driven books. His works span a range of topics, from personal development to leadership, violence prevention, and finding success. Josh holds a dual degree from the University of Colorado. He currently serves as the director of Out The Cage Academy and resides in Denver.

Acknowledgements

Writing a book is a process but it's been more rewarding than I could've ever imagined. None of this would be possible without the following amazing people—pushing me, guiding me, believing in me during this process—and I want to thank them.

First, there's Don Reynolds. Thank you for supporting, educating and mentoring me. Thank you for harvesting my potential and pushing me.

Sean White, "Always Purposeful, Never Flashy." Where do I start? Thank you for everything, always pouring into me. Making sure I'm doing what I'm supposed to. Thank you for informing me on many things I was "misinformed" about.

Josh Isom, (Iceman)! One of the hardest working man I know. Thank you! Thank you for always helping me when I'm lost or misinformed and leading me back the right way. Giving me advice and always encouraging me. Thankful to have you in my corner! You are important to the sports world. You inspire us all from sports to life.

Herman White, Jr. For the continuous support! Love is love, big bro!

Ms. Conley, (Aunt Nina) keep being amazing! Thank you for staying on me and pushing me. Chris Toombs, Thank you bro!

Jasmine McDonald. It's because of you that this book is possible. I appreciate you. Since we were kids, you've always encouraged me. Thank you for helping me. I am truly grateful. I appreciate you believing in me and my books. Thank you for making me better.

JR Jones. I appreciate you, bro. You've been my biggest supporter since day one!

I'm forever grateful to my Uncle Virgil and Aunt Dee.
They always informed me on the realities and inspired me
off and on the field. Educated me, taught me manners,
respect, and much more that has helped me succeed in life.

Coach Chris Warren. It's rare to meet someone who is
consistent and truly has a passion for helping others. Since
I was young, you've poured into me and have never given
up on me. Thank you for always motivating and always
supporting me. Thank you for setting the example. Thank
you for always sharing stories and teaching me the
importance of balance and being a great man. Thank you
for teaching me about the jimmies and joe in addition to
X's and O's"!

Halle Jones- We've talked throughout the process of this
book; the goal was to help these young athletes. Thank you
for the motivation and the understanding. You always
having my back. I'm truly grateful for you! Continue doing
amazing work in and outside the sports world.

Chris Young, Thank you, bro! You assisted with this
creation by always helping me better myself bro.

Phil Carter. Big bro, since day one, you've given me so
much game. Thank you for always looking out for me.
Buying my first pair of cleats for me and staying on me.
Kia Carter, I love you!

Desiree Frierson. Des, when you asked me to be a part of
your book a few years ago, I was motivated and it inspired
me. You showed me what's possible. Thank you for the
amazing work you do from the community, the youth,
family and the athletes. Thank you for your patience. Ron
Frierson and the family! Thank you for being persistent
with me and always bringing so much life.

Auri and Aurthur. You two have been amazing. The
constant critiques. I finally got this book out of my head
and onto paper, and I could never thank you enough.

Eric Bieniemy, thank you for helping me become a better man. Teaching me and guiding me. Thank you for always bringing the best out of me and for teaching me that "Good is the enemy of Great".

Eric Brown. Man from the basketball court, phone calls and chopping it up. I value it, bro. You always look out!

Justin Adams. You told me the world needed this book. I didn't think much of it, but you saw the vision!

Zach Lindsay. Bro, I'm forever grateful. You know the importance of this book and the topics in it. I appreciate you always, bro. Thank you for supporting me without hesitation.

Chris Andrews. Thank you for the constant support, bro. You've been through a lot, but you still make things happen. I appreciate you believing in me since day one! Bryce Andrews. You're a special kid, rare. You have a gift, a light... let it shine. Don't be afraid to be great. Your brother would be proud of you. Continue flourishing and being a great young man. Stay focused.

Nancy. For your amazing editing and feedback, I really appreciate you. Thank you for all the encouragement and dedication.

Narcy Jackson. The remarkable things that you've done are amazing, showing the athlete culture there is more to life. Your passion is second to none. Thank you for letting me be a part of it.

Duke.(Chance) Thank you for the revision and feedback. Thank you for the support and encouragement. It meant a lot and was a key component. Thank you for answering all my questions from *Out The Cage* to *Misinformed* and beyond—thank you for supporting me and my books.

Jason Anders. I appreciate you! thank you for the love and support bro.

CJ (Courtland) Thank you for all the love and support. Thank you for all you do, you a real one! #Misinformed love bro

Tia. The amazing work you do doesn't go unnoticed! From Colorado Xtreme, South High school and beyond. I appreciate you and all you do! Mentoring, educating, coaching and setting the example for young ladies everywhere. Nariah, Neveah and Naomi, continue to work hard and stay focused. I'm proud of you three. Keep being leaders and continue to accomplish all your goals.

Jamillah- Thank you for believing in me. Thank you for sharing, your amazing story. Thank you for serving and inspiring young people. Thank you for being humble, setting the example and being a leader!

So many people had a hand in bringing my hunger and Ambition to surface. The Entire PRO HUDDLE, My family, students and friends. Thank you for always pushing me and sticking with me through the highs and the lows.

For More Information:

Social Media

Twitter: @Beastmodeford

Instagram: @Beastmodeford

Instagram: @OutTheCage

Facebook: Mode Ford

ALSO AVAILABLE NOW!

Made in the USA
Lexington, KY
27 September 2019